GAGGLES
⟨OF⟩
GIGGLES

by Michelle Davila

Happy 1st birthday Chloe!

Love,
Jess

Apricot and Bee
2015

First Printing: 2015

ISBN 978-0-578-16418-2

Apricot and Bee, LLC

www.apricotandbee.com

Adam -

For the blanket capes you wear to dinner,
for packing only a sweater that time we went to Jamaica,
for being late to Thanksgiving because you were watching the alligators,
for pointing out birds and deer and squirrels and fireflies,
for picking wildflowers for me on our evening walks,
for keeping me young and in love,

This is for you.

Groups of animals
often have silly names.

They don't quite know why
(though they try to explain)!

A **shrewdness** of apes
grow sweet Concord grapes.

4

A **battery** of barracudas
stay cool in Bermuda.

A **sleuth** of bears
solve mysteries in pairs.

A **kaleidoscope** of butterflies -
clouds of color on the rise.

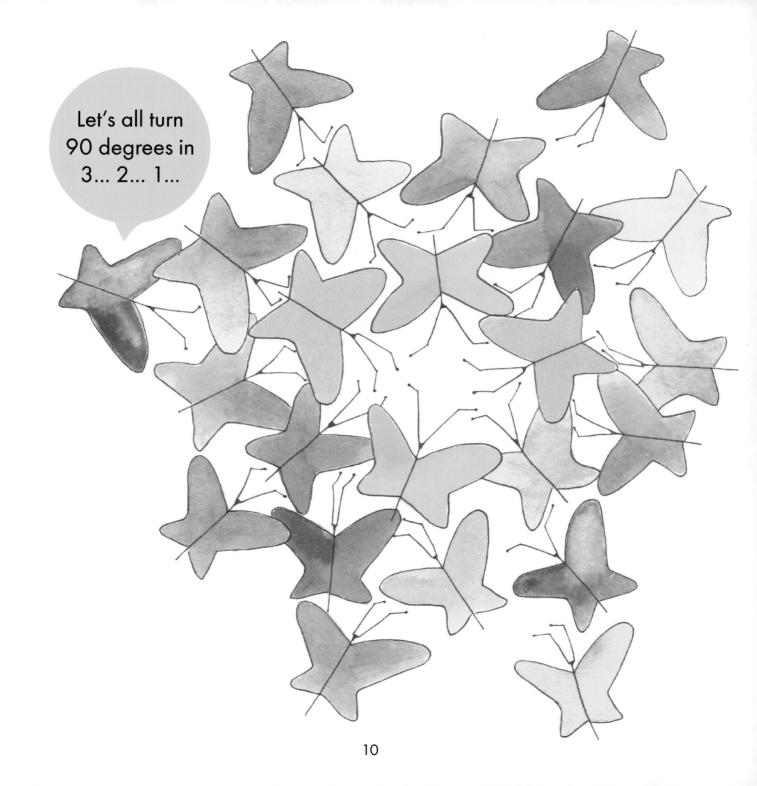

A **convocation** of eagles -
an assembly of legals.

A **charm** of finches -
quite polite in few inches.

A **flamboyance** of flamingos
like applause as they sing-o.

A **skulk** of foxes
will hide and flummox us.

A **gaggle** of geese
bring the beats, not the peace.

A **tower** of giraffes
have long necks and long laughs.

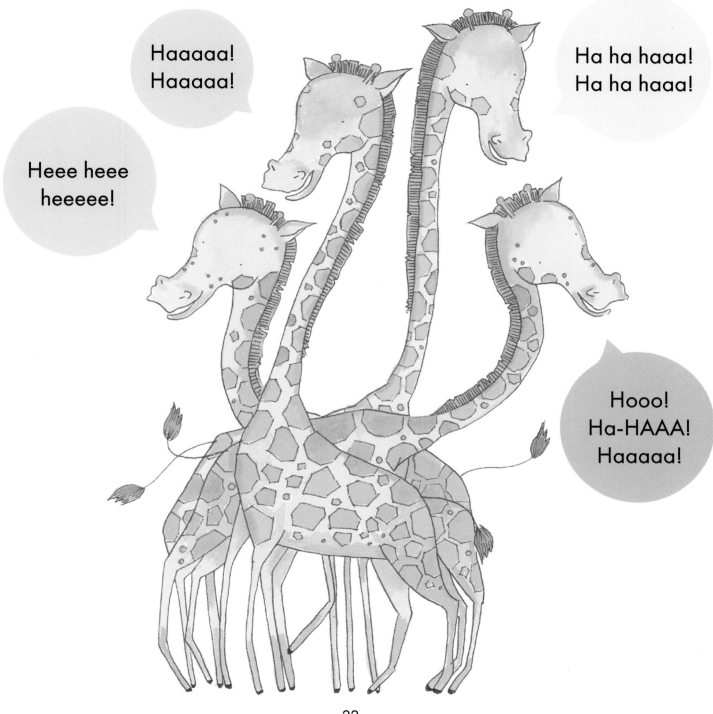

A **smack** of wild jellies
slurp peanut butter into their bellies.

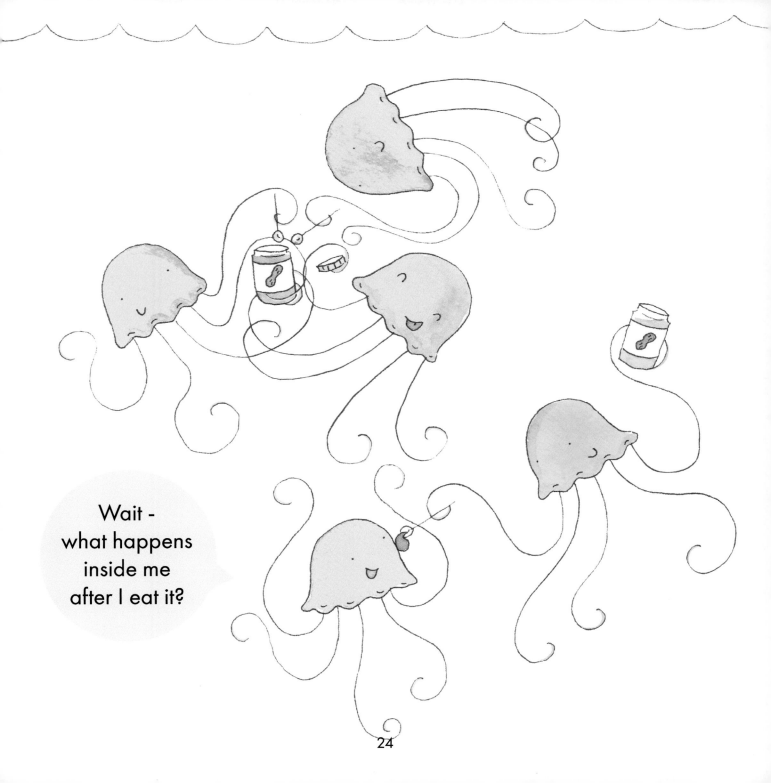

24

An **exaltation** of larks
fly merrily in arcs.

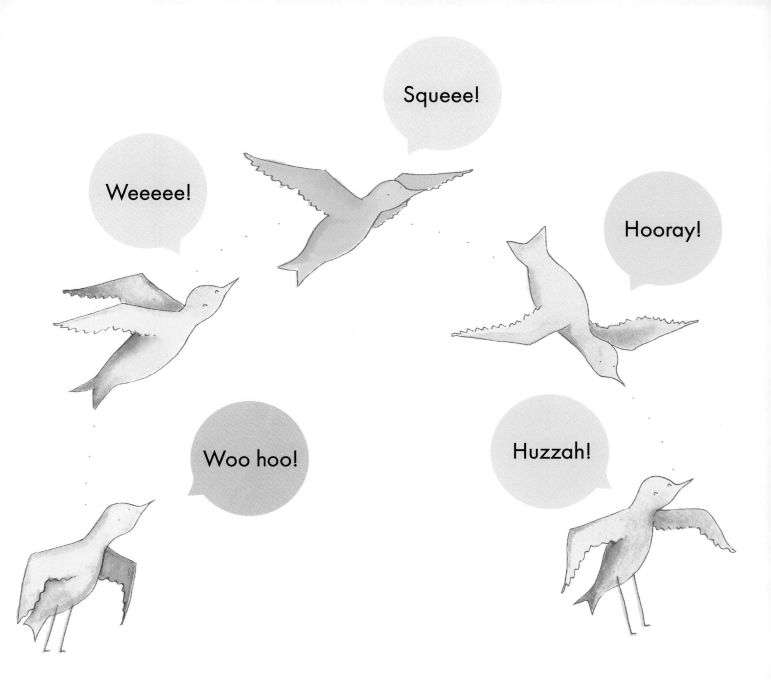

An **ostentation** of peacocks
wear pink hats and striped knee socks.

A **rookery** of penguins
nest together with their chins.

A **prickle** of porcupines
write letters with quill spines.

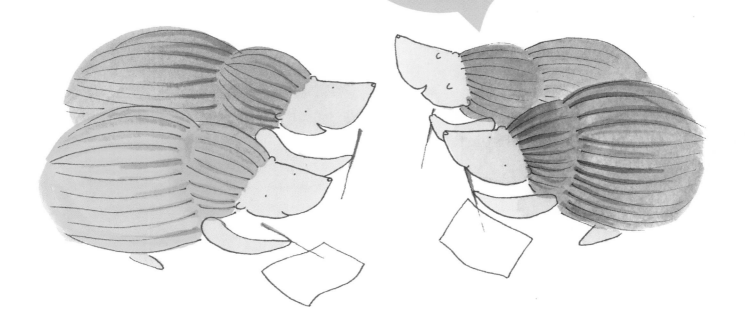

An **unkindness** of ravens
have faces quite graven.

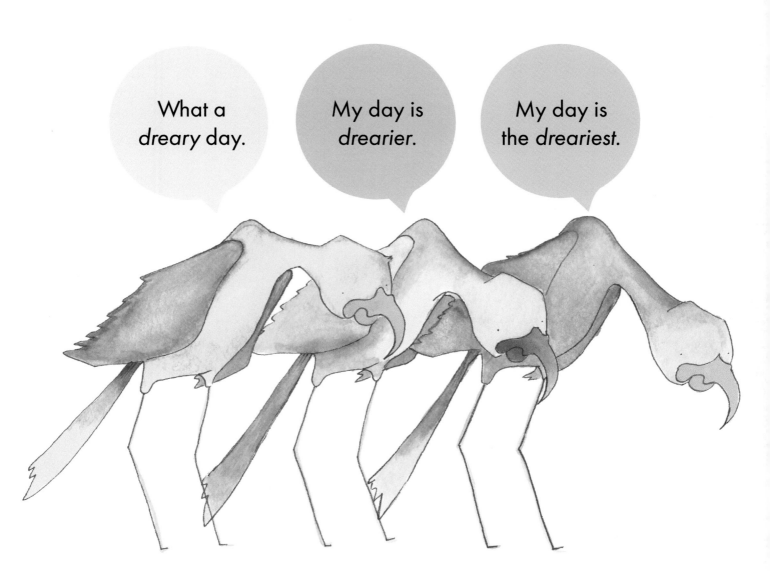

A **shiver** of sharks
get ready, on their marks!

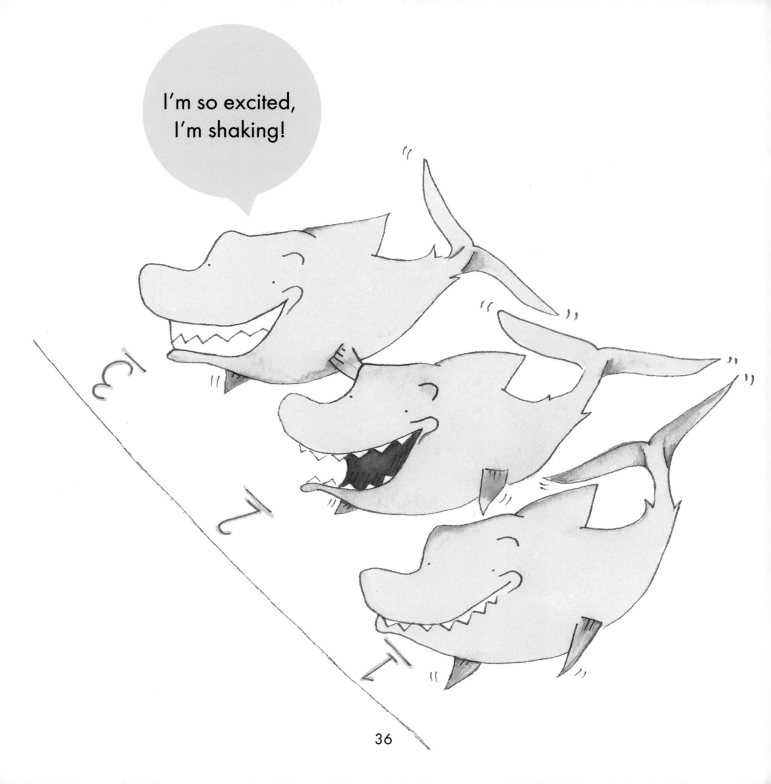

36

A **zeal** of zebras
feel wonders and see awes.

Life is just better
together - it's true.

Animal groups seem
to have more fun, too!